PENGUIN

THE HERMIT AND THE LOVE-THIEF

Bhartrihari was a philosopher of the fifth century AD. He is the author of *Śatakatraya*, a three part collection of Sanskrit poems about political wisdom, erotic passion, and renunciation. Popular stories portray Bhartrihari as a world-weary king who renounced society in bitter reaction to the infidelity of lovers. Another version, however, suggests that Bhartrihari was a Buddhist grammarian and yet others believe he was a courtier poet in the service of a king.

*

Bilhaṇa, the legendary author of the *Caurapañcāśika* (Fantasies of a Love-Thief) is known from his other writings as a poet who lived in the eleventh century AD and travelled throughout India to serve at various courts. According to legend, Bilhaṇa became involved in a secret affair with a king's young daughter whom he was supposed to be instructing in the subtleties of literature. When they were discovered, her father condemned him to death. In the moment before his execution he evoked the princess in fifty lyric verses whose beauty was so powerful that the goddess Kali interceded with the king to effect his pardon.

*

Barbara Stoler Miller is professor of Oriental Studies at Barnard College and one of the world's most renowned translators of the Sanskrit classics. Her books include *Love Song of the Dark Lord: Jayadeva's 'Gitagovinda'* and the *Ramayana.*

Bhartrihari and Bilhana

THE HERMIT
AND THE
LOVE-THIEF

Translated from the Sanskrit by
Barbara Stoler Miller

PENGUIN BOOKS

Penguin Books (India) Ltd., 72-B Himalaya House, 23 Kasturba Gandhi Marg,
New Delhi - 110 001, India
Penguin Books Ltd., Harmondsworth, Middlesex, England
Viking Penguin Inc., 40 West 23rd Street, New York, N.Y. 10010, U.S.A.
Penguin Books Australia Ltd., Ringwood, Victoria, Australia
Penguin Books Canada Ltd., 2801 John Street, Markham, Ontario, Canada L3R 1B4
Penguin Books (N.Z.) Ltd., 182-190 Wairau Road, Auckland 10, New Zealand

First published as *The Hermit and the Love-Thief* by Columbia University Press 1978
Published in Penguin Books 1990
Reprinted 1990
Copyright © Barbara Stoler Miller 1967, 1971, 1978, 1990

Made and printed in India by Ananda Offset Pvt. Ltd., Calcutta

This book has been accepted in the Indian Series of the Translations Collection
of the United Nations Educational, Scientific and Cultural Organization (UNESCO)

To Stella Kramrisch for teaching the ways of seeing

Contents

Preface

THESE TRANSLATIONS first appeared in separate collections entitled *Bhartrihari: Poems* (1967) and *Phantasies of a Love-Thief: The Caurapañcāśikā Attributed to Bilhaṇa* (1971). They have been revised and brought together here as outstanding examples of the classical Indian genre known as the fragmentary lyric. Each set of poems is amplified by a fascinating legend of the poet's life. These legends and their relevance to the poems of Bhartrihari and Bilhaṇa are the main subject of the introduction I have written for this volume. I hope that it will offer new readers of Indian poetry enough cultural and literary material to make the poetry more accessible and more enjoyable.

BARBARA STOLER MILLER

New York, 1978

A Note on Sanskrit Pronunciation

IN READING Sanskrit words, the accent is usually placed on the penultimate syllable when this is long; otherwise it is placed on the antepenultimate. A syllable is long if it contains a long vowel (*ā, ī, ū*), a diphthong (*e, o, ai, au*), or a vowel followed by more than one consonant. It should be noted that the aspirated consonants *kh, gh, ch, jh, th, dh, ph, bh,* and so on are considered single consonants in the Sanskrit alphabet.

Vowels are given their full value, as in Italian or German:

a	as *u* in c*u*t
ā	as *a* in f*a*ther
i	as *i* in p*i*
ī	as *i* in mach*i*ne
u	as *u* in p*u*t
ū	as *u* in r*u*le
ṛ	a short vowel; as *ri* in *ri*ver
e	as *ay* in s*ay*
ai	as *ai* in *ai*sle
o	as *o* in g*o*
au	as *ow* in c*ow*
ṃ	nasalizes and lengthens the preceding vowel
ḥ	a rough breathing, replacing an original *s* or *r;* lengthens the preceding vowel and occurs only at the end of a syllable or word

Most consonants are analogous to the English, if the distinction between aspirated and nonaspirated consonants is observed; for example, the aspirated consonants *th* and *ph* must never be pronounced as in English *th*in and *ph*ial, but as in ho*th*ouse and she*ph*erd. (Similarly, *kh*, *gh*, *ch*, *jh*, *dh*, *bh*.) The differences between the Sanskrit "cerebral" *ṭ*, *ṭh*, *ḍ*, *ḍh*, *ṇ*, and "dental" *t*, *th*, *d*, *dh*, *n* are another distinctive feature of the language. The dentals are formed with the tongue against the teeth, the cerebrals with the tongue turned back along the palate. Note also:

g   as *g* in *g*oat
ṅ   as *n* in i*n*k, or si*n*g
c   as *ch* in *ch*urch
ñ   as *ñ* in se*ñ*or (Spanish)
ś, *ṣ* as *sh* in *sh*ape or *s* in *s*ugar.

Certain words have been anglicized for the convenience of the reader, notably Bhartrihari (Bhartṛhari), Shiva (Śiva), Vishnu (Viṣṇu).

❧ INTRODUCTION ❧

IN INDIA, where the historical reality of ancient poets and even kings is elusive, poetry in the classical genre of the fragmentary lyric (*khaṇḍakāvya*) has usually been preserved anonymously. Despite this, several collections of miniature poems are attributed to known authors by the rich legendary traditions surrounding their names. Bhartrihari and Bilhaṇa are prominent in Indian literature for the quality of their poetry and the power of their legends.[1]

Bhartrihari was a philosopher of the fifth century A.D. He is the legendary author of the *Śatakatraya*, a three-part collection of Sanskrit poems about political wisdom, erotic passion, and renunciation. Popular stories portray Bhartrihari as a world-weary king who renounced society in bitter reaction to the infidelity of lovers. One version says that a brahman priest who had obtained a fruit of immortality decided to give it to his king, Bhartrihari. But the king gave it to his beloved queen, who gave it to her paramour, who in turn gave it to one of his mistresses, and she presented it again to the king. After reflecting for a time on this chain of events, the king cursed love and retired to the forest:[2]

> She who is the constant object of my thought
> is indifferent to me,
> is desirous of another man,
> who in his turn adores some other woman,
> but this woman takes delight in me.
> Damn her, damn him, the god of love,
> the other woman, and myself!

In an early written version of the Bhartrihari legend recorded by the Chinese pilgrim I-ching, who visited India in the seventh century, Bhartrihari is a Buddhist grammarian renowned for his continuing vacillation between the secluded life of a monk and the world of pleasure. In his epigrammatic poems of discontent Bhartrihari decries his own failure, fate, and the greedy inhabitants of his courtly world. The poet cannot choose between asceticism and worldly indulgence because he finds them equally attractive, and equally deficient. He dreams of finding salvation as a hermit meditating on Lord Shiva in a mountain cave washed by sprays of the sacred river Ganges, or lying embraced by Nature:

> Earth his soft couch,
> arms of creepers his pillow,
> the sky his canopy,
> tender winds his fan,
> the moon his brilliant lamp,
> indifference his mistress,
> detachment his joy—
> tranquil, the ash-smeared hermit
> sleeps in ease like a king.

The content of the verses, however, suggests that Bhartrihari was not a king but a courtier-poet in the service of a king. He makes frequent references to the degradation of a courtier's life and to the strained relationship between king and counselor. Bhartrihari is acutely sensitive to the lack of esteem for a poor poet in a materialistic society.

Bhartrihari's thoughts are those of a restless, frustrated man. He meanders, lingers nostalgically over trivial scenes, laments his wasted vigor and the tragedy of old age. He describes youthful women with the self-conscious lust of a lover who cannot trust that the attraction is mutual. He tells himself consolingly that his poetic art and wisdom are immortal, but he cannot escape the feeling that he has spent his youth vainly and that his life has been reduced to an overpowering greed. Compelled by a strong sense of personal irony, Bhartrihari sees man's position as paradoxical in a transient, seductive world.

Bilhaṇa, the legendary author of the *Caurapañcāśikā* ("Fantasies of a Love-Thief") is known from his other writings as a poet who lived in the eleventh century A.D. and traveled throughout India to serve at various courts. According to

legend, Bilhaṇa became involved in a secret affair with the
king's young daughter whom he was supposed to be instructing
in the subtleties of literature. When they were discovered, her
father condemned him to death. In the moment before his ex-
ecution he evoked the princess in fifty lyric verses whose beauty
was so powerful that the goddess Kālī interceded with the king
to effect his pardon. Each verse is a remembered moment of
love voiced in the first person by a separated lover who uses
memory to evoke his mistress's presence. Elegantly simple met-
aphors and sensuous compound adjectives describe her physi-
cal qualities and gestures of emotion:

> Even now,
> I remember her eyes
> trembling, closed after love,
> her slender body limp,
> fine clothes and heavy hair loose—
> a wild goose
> in a thicket of lotuses of passion.
> I'll remember her in my next life
> and even at the end of time!

Scattered references to "the princess" in these verses may
only be figures of speech, like other extravagant epithets Bil-
hana uses to characterize his mistress; the "I" of the verses
may only be a rhetorical device to intensify their emotional at-
mosphere. Nevertheless, it is impossible to separate the legend
from the content of the verses. The legend is a parable of the
pain and violence of frustrated love, which is paradoxically
aroused and overcome by remembering the joyous moments of
fulfillment. The formulaic *Caurapañcāśikā* verses sustain the in-
terplay between the antithetical moods of fulfilled and frus-
trated love that Sanskrit critics considered the height of aes-
thetic joy. The collection achieves its tone through the
threatening presence of death that plays over the cumulative
eroticism of the word-pictures.

Writers on Sanskrit poetry tend to stress its impersonality.
The British scholar A. B. Keith, for example, could detect no
revelation of personal character in the poems. When he com-
pared the Sanskrit poets to Sappho, Lucretius, and Catullus, he
found them wanting in vividness:

> They live moreover in a world of tranquil calm, not in the
> sense that sorrow and suffering are unknown, but in the
> sense that there prevails a rational order in the world
> which is the outcome not of blind chance but of the actions
> of man in previous births. Discontent with the constitution
> of the universe, rebellion against its decrees, are incompat-
> ible with the serenity engendered by this recognition by all
> the Brahmanical poets of the rationality of the world
> order. Hence we can trace no echo of social discontent; the
> poets were courtiers who saw nothing whatever unsatisfac-
> tory in the life around them. . . .[3]

Bhartrihari and Bilhaṇa both defy the stereotype, each in a
different way.

In both cases, the legends surrounding the verses are
mythical contexts for the poetry. The drama of its author's
legend makes the poetic personality of each collection more
vivid. The legends serve as parables indicating the dominant
poetic structures of the collections, in much the same way that
the prologue of a Sanskrit drama announces its dramatic struc-
tures. They explain the poetry by means that are different
from academic analyses of Sanskrit poetics, which character-
istically focus attention on the formal elements of individual
stanzas. The legends illuminate the human emotional basis of
the poetry, which the preoccupation with form obscures.

The mythic structure of each legend complements the con-
tent and language of the collected poems of Bhartrihari and
Bilhaṇa so well that it is possible to imagine that the legends
were self-consciously elaborated by the poets themselves. Tex-
tual evidence is against this in both cases. Once the verses and
the legends were associated, however, the legends clearly influ-

enced the literary history of the collections by making them distinct from eclectic anthologies. Verses in the anthologies were collected by critics and connoisseurs, just as miniature paintings are put in albums according to the taste of the collectors. They were culled mainly from older collections or from the Sanskrit dramas, and usually arranged to illustrate various poetic figures or themes.[4] In contrast, the collected poems attributed to Bhartrihari and Bilhaṇa are unified by their legends as well as by characteristic subject matter and formal devices.

The courts of ancient and medieval India delighted in eloquent speech. Words of counsel, as well as erotic and philosophical musings, were recited before the king in witty and elegant language. The poetic grace of the erotic verses of Bhartrihari and Bilhaṇa is obvious even in translation, but the sententious, reflective epigrams of Bhartrihari are not folksy bits of wisdom in verse form. They are also dominated by strict aesthetic technique and a self-conscious idea of art. When Bhartrihari regrets decline in the world he says:

> Wise men are consumed by envy,
> kings are defiled by haughty ways,
> the people suffer from ignorance.
> Eloquence is withered on my tongue.

The eloquence (*subhāṣita*) to which he refers is his own ability to compose the polished epigrams that characterize Sanskrit poetry.

"Sanskrit" means "refined" or "perfected." Applied to language, it implies a contrast with the Prākrits, the "unrefined" and more popular dialects that developed independently of the strict rules applied by the grammarian Pāṇini to the learned language of North India in about the fourth century B.C. Sanskrit was the hieratic language of the brahman priests, and by the time it entered court circles in the early centuries A.D. it was regularized and somewhat artificial—still highly inflected and abounding in complex constructions. Increasingly divorced

7

from the processes to which a natural language is subject, it was learned through a specialized training process and was employed mainly for official and literary purposes. It was a mark of distinction to have learned Sanskrit well, and the poets were masters of its intricacies.

The genre of Sanskrit lyric poetry within which Bhartrihari and Bilhana composed evolved from an ancient poetic tradition of hymn and epic. It is significant that both poets address their poems to particular divinities, from whom they seek favor. Bhartrihari directly invokes Shiva, the potent divine ascetic.[5] Bilhana ambiguously invokes Kālī when he remembers the princess. The epithets he uses could equally apply to the goddess or to his earthly mistress, making both of them the object of his prayer and the subject of his poems. Erotic poems thus become religiously powerful.[6] The exaggerated dramatic gestures of the poet's mistress suit her implied religious role as the incarnation of his muse and tutelary deity, who effects his salvation in response to the beauty of his poetry.

Invocations of the divine are characteristic of Indian poetry. The earliest preserved literature in India, the *Rig Veda*, expresses the notion that poetry is a means of establishing relations between the world of men and the world of the gods. In Vedic hymns, which were composed as invocations to accompany offerings poured on the sacrificial fire, speech is personified as a goddess (*Vāc*) who gives inspired priests the power to communicate with the world of the gods. By gaining insight into hidden correspondences between the human and divine realms, the seer-poet (*kavi*) attained the special power to give his visions concrete expression in poetry (*kāvya*). Fascination with expressing hidden correspondences between experience and imagination lies at the base of the metaphorical language that is exploited throughout the history of Indian poetry.

Because of the status of the *Rig Veda* as sacred revelation, classical Sanskrit poets and critics seem to have consciously avoided claiming it as the source of their poetic art. Instead they traced their craft to the post-Vedic epic *Rāmāyaṇa,* and named its traditional author, Vālmīki, the "first poet" (*ādikavi*).[7] A widespread popular legend tells that Vālmīki was a thief who became a sage by meditating on the word "death" (*māra*) until it became the name of the god Rāma (MA-RA MA-RA MA-RA-MA RA-MA RA-MA). By that time the sage was covered by an anthill (*valmīka*), from which he emerged as Vālmīki.

The text of the epic itself begins with a mythic dialogue between Vālmīki and the divine sage Nārada, who travels among men as a messenger of the gods. In answer to Vālmīki's inquiry about who in the world was the perfect man, Nārada outlined the story of Rāma, whose wife was abducted by a demon king. Obsessed by the story, Vālmīki went for a walk along the bank of the Tamasā river (which Rāma and his wife and brother crossed when they went into exile) and he saw a pair of cranes:

Nearby he saw a pair of birds innocently wandering—
The sonorous sound of mating cranes filled the forest.

But an evil-minded tribal hunter, hiding in a blind,
Shot the male of the pair while Vālmīki watched.

When his mate saw his bloody body writhing on the ground
Where it was struck, she cried a compassionate lament.

When the seer steeped in sacred law saw the bird
Shot by the hunter, compassion welled up in him.

Intense with compassion, he felt like the bird and saw,
"This act mocks sacred law." Hearing the crane's crying mate,
    he said:

"Hunter, year after endless year you will not find a place to
    rest,
For when these cranes mated you murdered the love-distracted
    male."

While he was speaking anxiety entered his heart.
"What is this I said—in such anguish for that bird?"

With great insight he continued to ponder.

Mindful, he made a design. Then the great sage said to his
  pupil:
"Divided into quarters of equal syllables measured to the lute's
  tempo,
Lyric verse came out of my anguish. Let verse so formed en-
  dure!"

This episode of the generation of lyric poetry from an-
guish is compressed in the Sanskrit into a half-pun on anguish
(*śoka*) and lyric verse (*śloka*). The episode is not only the frame
setting for the *Rāmāyaṇa*, but is at once a parable of poetic in-
spiration and a sample of the epic's pervading mood of com-
passion. As he walked on the riverbank, the whole anguish of
the Rāma story was fresh in his mind. It was revived by the
sound of the bird's cry at the death of her mate. The articu-
lated anguish of the female crane inspired Vālmīki to give ex-
pression to the anguish of the Rāma story in lyric verse. The
Indian tradition that framed its poetry in the mythical lives
of legendary poets was continuous from the time of the
Rāmāyaṇa.

Vālmīki's epic composition was the basis for both codified
genres of classical Sanskrit poetry, the narrative lyric (*mahā-
kāvya*) and the fragmentary lyric (*khaṇḍakāvya*). The *Rāmā-
yaṇa* remains throughout essentially an epic of oral literature,
characterized by redundancy of words and formulas and a pace
carefully measured to the listening audience, in which stanzas
flow into the narrative rhythm. Classical poetry, in contrast, is
characterized by brilliant condensation of independent stanzas,
metrical complexity, long compounds, and intricate figures of
speech.

Of the two genres, the narrative lyric is formally de-
scended from the ancient epic. Its conventions demand that it
be based on mythological or historical themes and that it con-
tain descriptions of mountains, moonrise, weddings, births, and
battles. Despite the rules that the syntax and imagery of indi-

vidual stanzas must be complete, verses were obviously conceived in groups meant to create the rich mood that is the aesthetic purpose of this poetry.[8] A vivid example of this genre is the opening of Kālidāsa's *Birth of the Prince,* which celebrates the love of the god Shiva for Pārvatī, the daughter of the Himālayas. Kālidāsa sets the scene by evoking the potent, sensuous divinity of the mountains:

Far in the north divinity animates the majestic mountain range
called Himālaya—a place of perpetual snow
that sinks deep into the seas on its eastern and western wings
and stands over the earth like a towering barrier.

Himālayan mountain high peaks hold a wealth of minerals
whose red glow diffuses through a cleft in the clouds
to produce an aura of untimely twilight,
making nymphs rush into evening ornaments.

Filling the hollow spaces of bamboo reeds
with winds rising from the mouths of caves,
Himālaya strives to sustain the droning tonic note
that celestial musicians need for their singing.

Himālayan herbs shine at night
deep inside cave shelters
where wild forest men lie with their rustic women—
herbs like lamps burning without oil to excite sensual love.

Bearing sprays from Ganges River waterfalls,
making cedar trees quake,
parting the peacocks' plume feathers,
Himālayan wind is worshipped by tribal hunters stalking deer.

Fragmentary lyric, the genre to which both Bhartrihari's and Bilhaṇa's collections belong, is defined in contrast to narrative lyric by its more restricted subject matter and by the independent quality of each stanza. Verses are neither bound together by narrative nor arranged into logical sequences. Each verse is grammatically complete and contains distinct images

11

and a dominant rhetorical device. The theoretical ideal is that an isolated verse should be appreciated on its own, without any larger context.

The verses are very short, most commonly quatrains in which the lines are structured into uniform, quantitative metrical patterns. The meters generally have fixed sequences of long and short syllables repeated in each quarter of the verse. As in Latin and Greek prosody, rhythm depends on the amount of time required to pronounce a syllable, not on stress.[9] The Bhartrihari collection contains twenty-one different meters, the most frequent of which have repeating sequences of syllables in the following patterns: *śārdūlavikrīḍitā* (19 syllables, - - - u u - u - u u u - / - - u - - u -); *śikhariṇī* (17 syllables, u - - - - - / u u u u u - - u u u -); *vasantatilakā* (14 syllables, - - u - u u u - u u - u - -). Bilhaṇa uses the meter *vasantatilakā* exclusively in his *Caurapañcāśikā*. The opening line of the poem scans according to its pattern:

adyāpi tāṁ kanakacampakadāmagaurīm
- - u - u u u - u u - u - -

Brevity is not poverty; abundant detail and great complexity of thought can be compressed into a simple metrical pattern. The miniature context is enriched by rhetorical ornamentation (*alaṁkāra*). The figures of speech commonly employed include many subtle varieties of metaphor, simile, allegory, synecdoche, antithesis, hyperbole, irony, and sarcasm. Consonant with the mocking opposition of worldliness to asceticism in the Bhartrihari legend, a tone of irony is present in many verses. This is effected by the frequent use of contrastive figures of speech, such as contradiction, objection, and rhetorical question.[10] Punning is a favorite technique of Sanskrit poetry. Though neither Bhartrihari nor Bilhaṇa uses it extensively, Bhartrihari's use of it (in verse 139) to strengthen the antithesis between passion and religious peace is a good example.[11] The sonorous qualities of chanted Sanskrit add to the verbal density of each verse. Rhyme is rare, but alliteration, assonance, and consonance are used freely. The miniature mold of each verse is expanded by poetic exploitation of the suggestive overtones (*dhvani*) of words and images. When words and images rich with connotations are used, they create multiple layers of meaning and thus intensify the aesthetic mood, *rasa,* of the poem.

The notion of *rasa* is at the heart of Sanskrit lyric poetry. The word is generally translated as "mood" or "sentiment," but it means more literally the taste or flavor of something—the *rasa* of a verse or a dramatic scene is the essential pervading flavor of a given emotional situation. Human emotion (*bhāva*), the basic material of *rasa,* is divided by the theorists into nine categories each of which has its corresponding *rasa* (the nine *rasas* are the erotic, the comic, the compassionate, the wrathful, the heroic, the terrifying, the loathsome, the marvelous, and the peaceful). The poet distills essential qualities from spontaneous emotion and structures them in order to awaken an aesthetic response in his audience of connoisseurs. In classical India new ideas, imagery, and techniques were less important than the skillful manipulation of conventional language. Literary conventions whose repetition may seem dull to us made their appeal to highly educated men of discriminating taste (*rasikas*) who were familiar with the techniques of the art and could attune themselves to the linguistic and expressive subtleties of Sanskrit. In a culture where the initiated audience relished poetry as much for its precious qualities as for the content of thought, conventional words and images were an important way of expanding meaning.

BHARTRIHARI'S POEMS

In India the life of a man is circumscribed by four traditional pursuits: *dharma* (righteousness, learning, and religious life), *artha* (material gain and political power), *kāma* (erotic love

13

and artistic pleasure), and *mokṣa* (the rejection of these three in order to concentrate on escaping from worldly bondage). In his poems Bhartrihari considers the relative merits of these pursuits. All are commended, but all are found deficient. Women and wealth breed anxiety; virtue and wisdom are rare and of little avail either in this world or in the forest; even the state of tranquillity, so arduously won, is threatened by sensuous beauty. Bhartrihari does not simply vacillate between wordly indulgence and asceticism; his confusion is more profound. He concurrently experiences delight in the fullness of the world, anxiety over its cruel transience, and the feeling that this tension is inescapable. His ironic sense that none of life's possibilities are what they seem gives pattern to his irreconcilable attractions and unifies the three parts of his collected poems.

Each section of the *Śatakatraya* concentrates on a different aspect of the poet's life: the *Nītiśataka* (here "Among Fools and Kings") expresses his worldly concerns and ideals; the *Śṛṅgāraśataka* ("Passionate Encounters") evokes his erotic moods and analyzes the nature of passionate love; the *Vairāgyaśataka* ("Refuge in the Forest") explores his disillusionment with the world and his thoughts on renunciation.

The *Nītiśataka*, like the popular Indian works of "good counsel," comments on man's obsession with acquiring wordly advantage and the obstacles he encounters. Yet its tone sets it apart from the didactic fables and aphorisms of works like the *Pañcatantra*. Many verses reveal a lurking attachment to the world as well as a revulsion against its sordidness. There is an undercurrent of turmoil and disenchantment to Bhartrihari's concern with worldly dominion and social action. He refers repeatedly to the intoxicating power of wealth, to insatiable greed, to unruly fate, to the haughtiness of kings, to the humiliation of servitude, to the supremacy of evil men in a society where virtue is judged only in terms of its proximity to gold. All this is very painful to a man who finds frank attraction in worldly pursuits and in life at court. He would prefer to grace

14

the summit of the world rather than to wither in the isolation of a forest retreat, but the world discourages him.

Concern with the power which greed and desire exert over man is a recurrent theme in Indian literature—Hindu, Buddhist, and Jain. Generally it is believed that desire, which is ultimately based on ignorance and delusion about the nature of things, is the source of every action—action which binds man to the suffering of continued existence in birth after birth. When Bhartrihari reflects on his own painful, perplexing position in the world of sense experience, he speaks of delusion, ignorance, desire, and bondage. The abstract terms have concrete and insidious meaning for him in the context of man's greed for material possessions and his passion for women.

If we see that Bhartrihari's erotic poetry expresses his subjugation to the power of desire, we shall find the verses of the *Śṛṅgāraśataka* less frivolous than they might otherwise seem. These stanzas possess depth and intensity precisely because the poet considers the confusion, longing, pain, and ephemeral pleasure of love to be at the center of human existence, implicit in any account of man's condition. Even in the verses about erotic love, Bhartrihari is more often intent on teaching life's absurd transience than on sustaining the classical mood of passion:

> Bearing the luster of a full moon
> at its loftiest phase,
> the lotus-face of a slender girl
> locks honey in her lips.
> What is tart now like unripe fruit
> on vines of gourd,
> when time has run its course
> will be an acrid poison.

Woman, his passion's object, is an enigma that defies Bhartrihari's solution. She seems to him an invitation to some kind of supraterrestrial paradise, but she is at the same time life's

15

device for enticing men into inescapable bondage. The delights of passionate encounter are at once beautiful and ominous; the vehemence of Bhartrihari's denunciation of woman is only a measure of the terrible fascination which she holds for him. The seductress who causes Bhartrihari's unrest is neither his wife nor a particular mistress, nor is she some idealized Beatrice; she is every woman who is young, affectionate, artful, charming, and voluptuous. His adoration of her is neither a worshipful nor a ritual love; it is concrete passion which delights in the physical subtleties of amorous play and in the seasons which set love's moods.

Emotion is not an isolated human phenomenon. The natural world of birds, flowers, and forests in their seasonal transformations expresses the emotions of man. The sensuous nuances of the changing natural world are evoked in Indian poetry to convey human dispositions. Bhartrihari expresses emotion amidst a multiplicity of sensuous qualities (colors, scents, sounds), and especially in his love poetry he tends to luxuriate in the richness which nature provides. This is not sparse poetry; the poet does not crystallize or unravel emotion. He rather tries to compress the profusion of its qualities into a flavor, into a thick, emotion-laden atmosphere so highly controlled that the audience shares in his experience.

Erotic emotion is magical, and magic is in the cycles of the seasons as well as in women's eyes. If Kāma, the god of love, has in woman a great weapon for subjugating man, in nature he has a powerful ally. The fragrances of freshly blooming flowers, breezes laden with sandalwood and rain, the sound of peacocks and cuckoos, the rays of the moon at its various phases all stimulate passion in a man. By their magic woman is transformed from a creature of flesh and bones into a siren who destroys man's reason.

Bhartrihari curses her not because she has become repugnant to him but because her beauty continues to lure him. He feels the need to tear himself away from the fetters of passion

INTRODUCTION

before old age overtakes him and his sensuality becomes a lecherous mockery of itself. But he is weak; he does not have the strength to renounce his erotic attachments in a world in which every movement serves to evoke both memory of some past pleasure and new longing.

Bhartrihari's bondage is complicated by his sense of the inevitability with which time ravages a man's life as the days and seasons revolve. Life and its pleasures are poisoned by the presence of time; and as he loses his capacity for pleasure, bondage in worldly existence becomes insufferable.

It is accepted in Indian belief that one's position in present life is rigidly determined by the net balance of good and bad actions in previous lives. If he accepts this doctrine of *karma* (action), Bhartrihari should be reassured. It seems to explain life's misfortunes as just results of past misdeeds, and seems to make man master of his future destiny. But one's *karma* is stored infinitely; it binds one, even if to better lives, to endless cycles of death and rebirth (*saṃsāra*). And the workings of *karma* are remote and abstract. Popular tradition pays lip-service to the doctrine of *karma* but turns to a notion of fate to provide a more ready explanation for the apparent absurdity with which *karma* expresses itself in the world. The concept of fate as it appears scattered through Bhartrihari's poems does not impair the validity of *karma* but operates on a different level: fate does not have the cosmic significance that *karma* does. Fate is invoked to explain the irrational confusion of events in the life of a man in society, frustrated by the pursuit of gain and concerned only with immediate results. He need not blame his own actions for his present state; his destiny is written on his forehead, having been traced there at the time of birth by a creator-god who acts by mere caprice.

Escape from the workings of fate and *karma* is theoretically possible through renunciation of the world, and this is the central subject of the *Vairāgyaśataka*. Bhartrihari longs for the dispassionate tranquillity of the forest, where he hopes to dwell as 17 an ascetic on the bank of a mountain river and pass his days in spiritual meditation. As in the erotic poetry, the emotions of man are associated with the natural world; here the calm mood of the forest reflects ascetic peace. In fact, Bhartrihari effects a strange transposition of the elements of an amorous scene into a convincing description of the tranquillity of a hermit in the forest. The hermit lies calm and happy in the embrace of nature almost as a lover lies weary after love-making in the arms of his mistress.

But though the quiet beauty of nature provides an environment conducive to meditation, it cannot assure the ascetic's release from the worldly bonds. In aesthetic consciousness the elements of sensuous experience are always present, no matter how transfigured. And their presence is potentially dangerous; the concentration of ascetics is threatened by woman's beauty. Even the great hermit-sages of legend (Viśvamitra and Riśyaśṛṅga in the *Mahābhārata,* Marīci in the *Daśakumāracarita,* divine Shiva) were enslaved by glances from a woman's eyes.

Release is possible only by overcoming time and the other worldly categories; only when his mind is absorbed in the equanimity of ultimate reality (*brahman*) can man cross beyond the ocean of *saṁsāra.* The practice of *yoga* and the pursuit of knowledge, which is discrimination, are means of escape. In all this Bhartrihari is expressing a concern with salvation which is the motivating force behind Indian philosophy; there is little thought here that is not expressed earlier in the Upanishads and *Bhagavad Gītā.* But there is uniqueness in the unorthodox juxtaposition of ideas to reinforce both the poet's own sense of suffering and his desire to escape it.

When he dwells in ignorance and is deluded by Love's magic, man sees the world filled with the glances of women, but when he achieves the state of dispassionate calm, his senses are disengaged and he rests in the pure vision of absolute reality— so the scriptures say. But this state is remote and the fortune of a very few men who possess extraordinary resolution. For the poet, indifference to women's eyes and falling blossoms seems impossible. The futility of the attempt is such that he cannot suppress the occasional feeling that the ascetic is a ludicrous figure. He is humanly skeptical about the possibility for salvation which tradition offers.

In terms of Bhartrihari's collected verses, man's life is an intricate web of conflicting moments and attractions. It is beautiful and pleasurable, but the beauty becomes bitter when he feels the weight of time and the caprice of fate upon him. His anxiety casts a gray shadow over pleasure and makes the world a prison house from which he sees no escape. Drunk with the wine of a little wealth or some passing enjoyment, a man is deluded by the world; though he experiences the transience of life, he cannot understand the real meaning of time or his own absurd position in it. Bhartrihari shows a keen awareness of the paradox involved in enjoining a deluded man to abandon the world of his delusion. Nevertheless, the life of a hermit remains for him the only way to step outside time and sever the bonds of worldly existence.

BILHAṆA'S POEMS

To anyone familiar with the conventions of Sanskrit poetry, there is nothing remarkable in Bilhaṇa's elegant catalog of remembered moments of love. But what is true of the individual verses does not hold for the *Caurapañcāśikā* collection. As one continues to read or hear the verses, the formulaic style and uniform meter serve to carry resonances from one verse to another. Images, descriptions, and dramatic scenes accumulate to produce a pervading and dominant mood of passionate love (*śṛṅgārarasa*). The particular mood of love expressed in the *Caura* is a blending of the ordinarily antithetical moods of love-in-separation (*vipralambha*) and love-in-enjoyment (*sambhoga*). By use of the formula "Even now" (*adyāpi*) and verbs meaning "I remember," "I see," "I meditate," the lover recreates their

19

love at the same time that he regrets their separation. The blending is not unique to the *Caura;* individual verses of this type are known from the anthologies.[12] What is unique is the repetition of "Even now" at the beginning of each verse, followed by a reference to the mistress, either by a pronoun or by synecdoche (e.g., *tad . . . vadanam,* that . . . face), followed in turn by some verb of remembering, often as the final element of the verse. The position of the verb does vary, and the act of remembering is also conveyed by indirect expressions which may appear anywhere in the verse. *Adyāpi* acts as a refrain, reminding the lover and the poet's audience that the details so vividly etched in his mind now belong to him only in his imagination. The intensive particle *api* (best translated as "even") emphasizes the present intensity of his passion and his wonder.

Between "Even now" and the word or phrase of remembering is the substance of the *Caura* verses, the lover's descriptions and characterizations of his mistress. Compound words, which are an important feature of the Sanskrit language, are exploited here to create the dense atmosphere. The majority of descriptive phrases in the verses are compounds of the type known as *bahuvrīhi.* Most of them can be read as string of adjectives and adjective phrases in English, with the final member serving as the base for the modifiers preceding it. Each compound taken as a whole functions as an epithet to delineate some characteristic of its subject. Although the poet's mistress is sometimes praised in abstractions, she more often emerges from a series of images that appeal directly to the senses. The sensuousness of the imagery is enriched by free use of alliterative sound patterns. A long compound, one of three in the fifth verse, illustrates the force of compound words and their sound symbolism. The half-verse reads:

adyāpi tāṁ surata-jāgara-ghūrṇamāna-
tiryag-valat-tarala-tāraka-dīrgha-netrām

The lines mean approximately: "even now her love-wakefulness-rolling-oblique-moving-glittering-pupils-long-eyes." Not only is this unsatisfactory in English, it is also less than the Sanskrit original conveys to its audience. Relationships of words in a compound are not explicitly indicated in Sanskrit, but the reader or listener is expected to be skilled enough to supply them. Usually the relationships are clear, but ambiguities are frequent, and these are used to expand the meaning of certain verses. A minor ambiguity exists in relating "rolling-oblique-moving-glittering-pupils" and "love-wakefulness"; are her pupils so agitated during love or because of it? The audience's interpretations will color this verse only slightly, but some cases are more extreme. A translation must retain the compression and sonority of the original:

> Even now,
> [I remember] her:
> deep eyes' glittering pupils
> dancing wildly in love's vigil.

These formal aspects of the *Caura* verses are all necessary to the production of the erotic mood, whose presence is greatly dependent on the poet's ability to construct an environment in which it can flourish. Seasonal changes of nature and descriptions of natural phenomena are commonly used to create an erotic flavor, as we saw in the poems of Bhartrihari. But these elements are notably absent in the *Caura*. Although the mistress is compared with birds, flowers, or the moon, there is no descriptive evocation of these. It is above all her manifestations of emotion, her movements, and her physical beauty that cause the excitement as they emerge in a web of sensuously descriptive, sonorous words.

The lover recaptures his mistress through her responses to love. Emotional reactions are shown by their external manifestations (*anubhāva*) in her eyes, face, limbs, and gait. For example, shame can be inferred from the fact that she cowers to cover her body or lowers her face. Such emotional responses are classed by the Sanskrit critics as transitory states of emotion (*vyabhicāribhāva*), which function in cooperation with the pervading emotional state (*sthāyibhāva*)—as it were, emerging from it and being submerged in it, like waves in the ocean. The transitory states not only change, they rarely occur simply and are usually combinations of the psychological states of anxiety, fear, shame, modesty, anger (real or feigned), affected indifference, sorrow, and fatigue.

The physical responses to love are largely involuntary manifestations of emotion (*sattvabhāva*). Indian aesthetic theory considers them highly significant because they arise from inner feeling and cannot be simulated. In the love situation such signs as sweating and bristling of the hairs on the skin show the body's natural excitement and longing, no matter what one may do to pretend otherwise. Also taken as involuntary signs are paralysis, trembling, weeping, change of color, breaking of the voice, and fainting. Physical beauty is thought to be enhanced by the signs, and few descriptions of beauty ignore them. Concrete images of sounds, odors, tastes, and textures supplement the visual imagery and heighten the sensuous appeal of the poetry.

Bilhana's poems, unlike the epigrammatic verses of Bhartrihari, lend themselves well to visual interpretation. A series of miniature paintings was done in the sixteenth century to illustrate Bilhana's work.[13] Formal and symbolic means are exploited in the paintings to concentrate the viewer's attention on the relationship between the central female figure, which appears in every painting, and the male figure of Bilhana. The elaborately painted figures, like the princess and her lover in the poems, are drawn in stylized movements, presented to stimulate the response of a cultivated audience.

NOTES

1. Scholarly research in Indian textual criticism has made it increasingly reasonable to identify Bhartrihari, the traditional author of the *Śatakatraya* poems, with the fifth-century philosopher-grammarian who wrote the treatise entitled *Vākyapadīya* and to identify the author of the *Caurapañcāśikā* poems with the eleventh-century poet who wrote the literary epic entitled *Vikramāṅka-devacarita*. In both cases the identifications are made on the basis of known legendary material and subject matter common to the lyric verses and the other works.

D. D. Kosambi, in the introduction to his critical edition of *The Epigrams Attributed to Bhartrihari* (*Bhartṛhari-viracitaḥ Śatakatrayādi-subhāṣitasaṃgrahaḥ*, Bombay, 1948), notes the impossibility of reconstructing a definitive text on the basis of the extensive manuscript material he examined, but he did find it remarkable that in spite of the extraordinary variation from version to version, the total impression produced by any of them is about the same. He concludes, "A certain type of stanza came to be attracted to the collection . . . the seeds must necessarily have been present in the original collection to permit such growth." The group of 200 stanzas which Kosambi determined to be most authentic by the criteria of textual criticism, and which constitute the text for my translation, do echo a tone of irony, skepticism, and discontent which is unique in Sanskrit literature. The poetry of Bhartrihari shares with the grammatical philosophy of Bhartrihari, as expounded in the *Vākyapadīya*, ideas and terminology drawn from traditional systems of Vedānta and Saṅkhya metaphysics, as well as from classical Yoga psychology. Also common to the poetry and the philosophy is a critical interest in the nature of time. In Bhartrihari's philosophy, time is a creative power that is responsible for the birth, continuity, and destruction of everything in the universe. Much of the poetry shows a pessimistic preoccupation with the beginning and end of things. The inevitability with which time is said to ravage the life of man may conceivably represent the poetic expression of the futility and dejection attendant upon a philosopher profoundly impressed by the power of time. Good arguments are put forth to date Bhartrihari the philosopher to the fifth century A.D. The core of the collected poems attributed to Bhartrihari also probably dates to this period. Although the oldest preserved version of the *Śatakatraya* text took form in the eleventh or twelfth century, there is good evidence that the collection existed in some form long before this.

The Chinese pilgrim I-ching, in his *Record of the Buddhist Religion as Practised in India and the Malay Archipelago: A.D. 671–695* (trans. J. Takakusu, Oxford, 1896), wrote that a grammarian named Bhartrihari, author of the *Vākyapadīya* and another work which "treats of the principles of human life as well as of grammatical science," died in A.D. 650. Although I-ching's dating is inaccurate, his account of Bhartrihari's vacillation between the Buddhist monkhood and the life of sexual indulgence, about which Bhartrihari is said to have composed stanzas, suggests that at the time I-ching traveled in India, Bhartrihari was already a legendary figure. For details of the scholarly arguments see Kosambi, *Epigrams,* pp. 78–81; Daniel H. H. Ingalls, *An Anthology of Sanskrit Court Poetry* (Cambridge, Mass., 1965), pp. 41–43; K. A. Subhramania Iyer, *Bhartṛhari* (Poona, 1969), pp. 1–15, 110–31; H. G. Coward, *Bhartṛhari* (Boston, 1976), pp. 11–12, 95–104. The identification of the *Caurapañcāśikā* poet with the Kashmiri author of the *Vikramāṅkadevacarita* is based on his legend and on textual analysis of the two works. In two versions of the legend, which accompany the *Caurapañcāśikā* poems in many manuscripts, Bilhaṇa is described as a master-poet who was called to the court of a king to instruct the king's nubile daughter in the subtleties of literature. Little is said in the legends about the poet himself; the stories dwell on his relationship with the princess, the discovery of their liaison, his condemnation to death, and his pardon. In the *Vikramāṅkadevacarita,* Bilhaṇa devotes the entire last chapter (XVIII) to an account of his life, his country of origin, and his travels. What is of interest here is his description of his grand tour (XVIII.86–102, translated in my *Phantasies of a Love-Thief,* p. 189), which culminates in his appointment to the position of court-poet (*vidyāpati*) at the court of the Chalukya king Vikramāditya VI (A.D. 1076–1127). The route he describes is of particular interest because he notes the various courts which he visited and at which he defeated other poets with his verses. Although he makes no mention of the exact content of his verses, he suggests that he was given to composing poems about beautiful women (XVIII.100).

There is marked similarity in style and content between verses of the *Caurapañcāśikā* and verses in the eighth section of the *Vikramāṅkadevacarita* describing King Vikramāditya's bride, Candralekhā. In both works physical details are elaborated to present a picture of the beloved girl. For further evidence supporting Bilhaṇa's authorship of both works, see *Phantasies of a Love-Thief,* pp. 2–7, 188–91.

2. See *Vikrama's Adventures,* trans. by Franklin Edgerton (Cambridge, Mass., 1926), pp. 5–14, "King Bhartṛhari and the fruit that gave immortality."

3. *A History of Sanskrit Literature* (Oxford, 1928), p. 345.

4. A superb example of the Sanskrit anthology is the *Subhāṣitaratnakoṣa,* edited by D. D. Kosambi and V. V. Gokhale (Cambridge, Mass., 1957), trans. by Ingalls, *Sanskrit Court Poetry.* A modern example of a connoisseur's anthology is *Sanskrit Love Poetry,* trans. by W. S. Merwin and J. Moussaieff Masson (New York, 1977).

5. To appreciate the affinities between Bhartrihari and the god he worships, see Wendy O'Flaherty, *Asceticism and Eroticism in the Mythology of Śiva* (London, 1973).

6. This kind of ambiguity is characteristic of Indian medieval literature; see, for example, my *Love Song of the Dark Lord: Jayadeva's Gītagovinda* (New York, 1977).

7. Summarized from my article on the legendary origin of poetry in India; see "The Ādikāvya: Impact of the *Rāmāyaṇa* on Indian Literary Norms," *Literature East-West,* 17, nos. 2–4 (1973), 163–73. A comparison between the *Rāmāyaṇa* and the *Mahābhārata* frame episodes is illustrative of the basic differ-

ences between the two epics. The traditional author of the *Mahābhārata* is Vyāsa, the sage grandfather of the Pāṇḍavas; he is "a celebrated compiler of the Vedas." Vyāsa tells the story of the battle he saw with his own eyes and the story is narrated by one of his disciples, the priest Vaiśampāyana, at an assembly of warriors come together for the snake sacrifice being held by Janamejaya, a descendant of the Pāṇḍavas. It is then retold by court bards (*sūtas*) in a narrative delivery. (See J. A. B. van Buitenen, translator, *The Book of the Beginning, The Mahābhārata*, vol. 1, Chicago, 1973.) Vālmīki is represented by the tradition that looks to him as the author of the *Rāmāyaṇa* as a poet, in the line of Vedic seer-poets, who was inspired by compassion to compose the Rāma story in lyric verse. The rhapsodists (*kuśīlavas*) learned the poem from Vālmīki and sang it before Rāma himself. This position of the rhapsodists in contrast to the court bards is significant for the shape and style of each epic, one essentially an epic poem of emotion, the other essentially an epic narrative of heroic deeds.

8. See Ingalls, *Sanskrit Court Poetry*, p. 34; Edward C. Dimock, et al., *The Literatures of India* (Chicago, 1974), pp. 152–56.

9. For a more detailed discussion of Sanskrit prosody, see my *Love Song of the Dark Lord*, pp. 9–10, 43–47 (notes 8–21). The moric meter *āryā* is also used by Bhartrihari.

10. See Edwin Gerow, *A Glossary of Indian Figures of Speech* (The Hague, 1971); note the figures of contradiction called *virodha, ākṣepa, praśna*.

11. *keśāḥ saṃyaminaḥ śruter api param pāram gate locane*
    antarvaktram api svabhāvaśucibhiḥ kīrṇam dvijānām gaṇaiḥ
    muktānām satatādhivāsaruciram vakṣojakumbhadvayam
    ittham tanvi vapuḥ praśāntam api te rāgam karoty eva naḥ

Pun Words	Passion	Peace
samyamina	tied-up (hair)	self-control
param pāram gate	extended (to ear); i.e., long (of eyes)	gone to the opposite shore of worldly existence
śruti	ear	Vedas
dvijāna	teeth	twice-born man; one who is initiated
mukta	pearl	released; liberated from worldly existence

Quite impossible to render by punning in English!

12. Verses 786, 787, 788 of the *Subhāṣitaratnakoṣa* are similar to the *Caurapañcāśikā* form; see Ingalls, *Sanskrit Court Poetry*, pp. 242, 248–49.

13. The extant paintings are reproduced and analyzed in *Phantasies of a Love-Thief*, pp. 202–33. A single example is on the cover of this book.

❧ BHARTRIHARI'S POEMS ❧

Among Fools and Kings
Passionate Encounters
Refuge in the Forest

Prologue

1

Radiating uncanny light
from the crescent moon crowning his head,
blazing his fire of bliss
to consume the moth of frenzied love,
dispelling dismal clouds of delusion
by hurling his thunderbolt to the heart,
Shiva triumphs—wisdom's lamp
deep inside the ascetic's mind.

2

Gaunt, blind, lame, shorn of ears and tail;
mangled, putrid, covered with worms;
starved, wizened, wearing an alms bowl shard
on his neck—a dog will still follow a bitch.
Passion smites even those bereft of life.

3

Refrain from taking life,
never envy other men's wealth,
speak words of truth,
give timely alms within your means.
Keep silent on the conduct of women,
dam the torrent of your craving,
do reverence before the venerable,
and bear compassion for all creatures—
this unerring path to bliss
is taught in all the texts of scripture.

4

Wise men are consumed by envy,
kings are defiled by haughty ways,
the people suffer from ignorance.
Eloquence is withered on my tongue.

5

When I knew but a little, I was blinded by pride,
as an elephant is by rut;
with my mind so stained I believed,
"I am a sage."
But slowly I learned from the presence of men
wise in myriad ways;
my pride, like fever, was subdued and I knew,
"I am a fool."

6

When dark passion wove
a web of ignorance about me,
then a woman seemed
to fill the world's expanse.
But now that I am favored with
keener discernment,
my tranquil sight sees Brahman
throughout the universe.

7

A splendid palace, wanton maids,
and a white umbrella's princely luster
are luxuries of wealth that survive
only while auspicious karma thrives.
When this is exhausted then wealth,
like a string of pearls snapped
in violent games of love,
is squandered—
falling in every dark direction.

Among Fools and Kings

8

An ignorant man is readily pleased;
more readily yet is a sage.
But a man corrupted by trifling knowledge,
Brahmā himself cannot sway.

9

A man may tear a jewel
from a sea monster's jaws,
cross a tumultuous sea
of raging tides,
or twine a wrathful serpent
garland-wise on his head.
But no man can please
the mind of an obstinate fool.

10

The moon paled by day,
a loving woman's lost youth,
a lake without lotuses,
the dumb face of a handsome man,
a prince obsessed with wealth,
a man of virtue perpetually wretched,
a villain come to the court of a king—
seven barbs in my heart.

11

A gem carved by the jeweler's stone,
a warrior-hero wounded at arms,
an elephant wasted by rut,
river banks dry in the sultry months,
the moon in its final phase,
a girl exhausted by loveplay,
and men whose riches are spent in alms—
all are magnificent in their decline.

12

A hungry man craves a handful of barley,
but sated he deems the whole earth straw.
It is the condition of men's fortunes
that exaggerates or belittles things.

13

Their speech is rich with words of scripture,
their learning is worthy of students:
when wise men are poor in a king's domain,
the ruler shows his folly.
Even in poverty sages are lords;
vulgar appraisers are open to censure—
not the jewels they cheapen.

14

Courage in adversity, patience in prosperity,
eloquence in assembly, heroism at arms,
delight in fame, devotion to scripture—
all are in the nature of noble men.

15

It eludes thieves' pillage,
promotes endless joy;
bestowed on those who beg,
it still increases
and never perishes with time.
Wisdom is a deep treasure.
Kings, give up this arrogance
toward its masters!
Who can rival them?

16

Do not scorn the men
who have won supreme truth;
worthless as straw to them, wealth
offers no temptation.
Elephants with streaks of rut
staining their temples
are not restrained
by filaments of a lotus stalk.

17

Even starved, weakened by old age,
fallen to a wretched state,
plagued by faded power,
his life breaths ebbing away—
when he longs for a morsel torn
from the temple of an elephant in rut,
how can the lion, proudest of creatures,
stoop to feed on withered grass?

18

A man should choose judicious ways,
shun treachery even at peril of death;
neither supplicate evil men
nor beg alms of an indigent friend;
hold his head high in the face of misfortune,
and walk in the footsteps of great men.
Who revealed to the saints this vow
as severe as a sword's bare blade?

19

Men whose thoughts and words and deeds
are steeped in the nectar of merit,
who fill the world's expanse
with a flood of benevolent acts,
build into august mountains
the granules of other men's graces,
and spread abroad their own heart's joy—
such saintly men are few.

20

Bearing Vishnu's sleeping form,
holding the host of his foes at bay,
sheltering winged mountains seeking
refuge from the demons' wrath,
enduring the infernal fire
with all its voracious flames of doom—
fathomless is the burden
weighing on the ocean's ample body.

21

He may sleep on bare ground or on a couch,
fare on roots or dine on sweet rice,
wear rags or heavenly robes;
when he knows his goal, a wise man
pays no heed to pain or pleasure.

22

We would bow to the gods,
but even they submit to destiny.
We would pay destiny homage,
but it can only grant reward
in accord with our karma.
If karma is the source of all reward,
what use are gods or destiny?
Our allegiance is to karma,
which even destiny does not control.

23

Beware!
Kings are ruined by bad advice,
ascetics by society,
offspring by indulgence,
priests by ignorance of scripture,
a family by degenerate sons,
morality by bad company;
modesty by wine,
husbandry by lack of care,
affection by distance,
friendship by distrust,
prosperity by lack of luck,
and wealth by prodigal ways.

24

Apathy is ascribed to the modest man,
fraud to the devout,
hypocrisy to the pure,
cruelty to the hero,
hostility to the anchorite,
fawning to the courteous man,
arrogance to the majestic,
garrulity to the eloquent,
impotence to the faithful.
Does there exist any virtue
which escapes
the slander of wicked men?

25

Cast noble birth to hell!
All the virtues even lower!
Throw morality down a mountain,
and lineage into a fire to burn!
Let thunderbolts strike hostile valor!
Leave us free to win that wealth
without which all these merits
count as worthless bits of straw!

26

A mouse gnawing a hole in a basket fell
through it at night into the mouth of a serpent
whose despondent body lay cramped
in the basket; hunger had weakened his senses.
But nourished by the mouse's flesh,
he escaped by the very same passage.
Be content! Chance alone confounds
the rise and fall of men.

27

One should avoid an evil man
even if knowledge adorns him.
Is not a diamond-hooded serpent
an agent of danger?

28

In mixture with water
the substance of milk is diluted.
Water, feeling milk's burning pain,
yields itself to the fire's attack.
Then to relieve the plight of its friend
milk becomes willing to burn.
But mixed again with water, milk is calmed.
Compare to this the friendship of good men.

29

In an instant she makes evil men good,
foolish men wise, enemies affectionate,
the unknown perceptible, poison ambrosia.
So celebrate the goddess of virtue
and savor her cherished fruits.
Do not waste effort, good man,
in vain pursuit of too many merits!

30

With relish due ambrosia, a dog eats a meatless bone,
wormy, spittle-wet, putrid, and vile. He would eat
without qualm even if he saw the lord of gods nearby.
A wretch does not assess the poverty of his lot.

31

He wards off sin and urges
more auspicious ways;
conceals your secrets
and sings aloud your virtue;
never retreats in time of need,
but rather offers aid.
The sages so describe
the marks of a worthy friend.

32

The deer, the fish, and the good man
only care for grass or sea or peace.
The hunter, the fisherman, and the cynic
are their wanton enemies on earth.

33

A piercing hiss augurs swift end
of a drop of water touching molten iron,
but a drop resting on a lotus-leaf
assumes a mellow pearl-like hue.
And if in light of some auspicious star
it falls into an oyster shell, it turns into a pearl.
And man attains to vile or mean
or lofty ways through the company he keeps.

34

Like clusters of blossoms,
wise men have two destinies:
to grace the summit of the world
or wither in the forest.

35

When silent, the courtier is branded dumb;
when eloquent, pretentious or a prating fool;
when intimate, presumptuous;
when distant, diffident;
when patient, pusillanimous;
when impetuous, ill-bred.
The rules of service are a mystery
inscrutable even to masters of wisdom.

36

Rising through humility,
telling their own merits
by praising the merits of others,
achieving personal ends
with arduous tasks
on behalf of other men,
shaming the abusive spate
of evil men's invectives
with simple acts of patience—
saints who perform such miracles
are highly esteemed in the world.
Who would not revere them?

37

Where there is greed, what need of other evil,
where calumny, of other sin?
Where there is truth, what need of penance,
where pure mind, of pilgrimage?
Where there is amity, what need of allies,
where grandeur, of ornaments?
Where there is wisdom, what need of wealth,
where infamy, of death?

38

The capricious disposer of fate may destroy
the lotus-bed play of a wild goose.
But he can never steal the fame of its skill
in separating water from milk.

39

A bald-headed man, his pate
burned by the sun's rays,
desiring a shady spot, went by fate
to the foot of a wood-apple tree.
And there his head was smashed
by a large falling fruit.
Wherever a luckless man goes,
adversities follow him there.

40

No fruit is borne by beauty's charm,
or noble birth, or moral conduct,
or knowledge, or service done
with arduous care.
Only fortune's merits,
amassed from former penances,
in season bear their fruit for man,
as do the trees.

41

Kindness is an ornament for power,
restrained speech for valor,
dispassion for wisdom,
discipline for tranquillity,
munificence for wealth,
forbearance for austerity,
patience for majesty,
and candor for duty—
but moral conduct, the cause of all,
is a gem that crowns the rest.

42

It destroys the mind's folly,
pours truth into speech,
bestows esteem's rare majesty;
drives out sin,
purifies the thought of man,
and spreads his fame across the skies.
What can't wise company
do for a man?

43

Men are rare who have
desire for good company,
joy for the merits of others,
humility towards the venerable,
zealous yearning for knowledge,
affection for their wedded wives,
fear of slander in the world,
devotion to trident-armed Shiva,
power of self-control,
immunity from evil ties.
We pay our deepest homage
to these saints of spotless virtue!

44

Drown your raging thirst, cultivate patience,
conquer wanton pride and your mind's obsession with sin!
Speak the truth, follow straight the sanctioned way,
pay service at the feet of learned men!
Revere the worthy, pacify your foes,
envelop your virtues in modesty's cloak!
Guard your good name, and console wretched creatures!
This is behavior which marks noble men.

45

Before he implements any act,
be it villainous or good,
a wise man will weigh with care
all possible repercussions.
The fruition of actions
performed with impetuous haste
is like a poisoned arrow,
tormenting man's heart unto death.

46

In dark forests, in war,
amid fiends or floods or fires,
in vast oceans or on high peaks,
sleeping or courting danger
with reckless abandon—
merits earned in former lives
afford a man protection.

47

Dreadful forests become princely towns for him,
rare friendship is offered to him by all men,
and earth becomes his mine of precious gems—
a man's former noble deeds give rich reward.

48

Dive if you will into fathomless seas,
ascend Mount Meru's peaks,
vanquish enemies at arms;
acquire skill in tillage and trade,
gain mastery of the sciences
and varied arts;
or endeavor with effort stupendous
to travel through the vast skies
like a bird.
You may do all this, but karma's force
alone prevents what is not destined
and compels what is to be.

49

Indra's guide was the divine priest,
his weapon the thunderbolt,
his army the gods, his citadel heaven,
his ally Vishnu, his elephant primordial—
even Indra, slayer of dreadful demons,
endowed with extraordinary prowess,
was broken in battle by militant foes.
No power gives refuge from fate.
How vain are all efforts of valor!

50

Generosity, luxury, and ruin
all reduce a man's wealth.
A miser, who neither gives nor enjoys,
lives in dread of the third.

51

A man of wealth is held to be high-born,
wise, scholarly, discerning;
eloquent, and even handsome—
all virtues are accessories to gold!

52

The gods were not appeased by the fabulous gems
they drew from the cosmic ocean;
nor did they falter when the sea spewed forth
a dreadful poison.
They ceased to churn its milky waters
only when it yielded up
the nectar of immortal life.
The resolute never relinquish their goal.

53

Some will grant the orbiting planets
claim to high regard,
but the demon Eclipse, who tasted power
in the divine elixir, will not battle them.
This demon prince, whose severed head
is his souvenir of Vishnu's wrath,
reserves his revenge for a special pair—
at a fixed celestial time he swallows
the luminous lords of night and day.

54

The ear of a compassionate man
is graced by the scriptures,
not by pendants;
his hand by bounty,
not by bracelets;
his body by benevolence,
not by sandal paste.

55

Victorious are the favored master-poets,
skilled in the sentiments' alchemy.
In their body of fame they feel
no threat of old age, death, and rebirth.

56

Whatever wealth, vast or small, is traced
on man's brow by Brahmā, disposer of fate,
he will find in a barren desert—
no more on golden Mount Meru.
Be patient then! Do not waste your effort
in servile conduct before the rich!
See, the jug draws the same amount
of water from a well or from the sea.

57

Wagging his tail, crouching to beg,
writhing through ridiculous tricks,
a dog toadies to the hand that feeds him,
while the lordly elephant-bull
views all with aloof disdain and devours
his food while others bear him flattery.

58

King, if you wish to milk your realm like a cow,
first nourish the world as you would a calf.
When it is nurtured with constant care,
a kingdom yields fruits like a wish-granting vine.

59

Sincere and fraudulent,
harsh and honey-tongued;
ruthless as well as merciful,
niggardly, then munificent;
at one time prodigal,
at another miserly with his hoards of wealth—
kingly behavior, like a harlot,
shows infinite variety.

60

No man is the favorite
of a king inclined to passionate rage.
A fire when touched burns even the priest
who pours it oblation.

61

Want of compassion, wanton pugnacity,
plunder of other men's wealth and wives,
impatience with good men and kinsmen alike;
all are in the nature of wicked men.

62

One begins large, shrinking in time,
the other, small at first, later expands.
As shadows of afternoon and morning differ,
so differs the friendship of evil and good men.

63

Boughs bend low with ripened fruit;
clouds hang down with fresh rain;
noble men bow graciously with riches.
This is the way of bountiful things.

64

The sun brings pools of lotuses to bloom,
the moon illuminates nocturnal lilies,
a cloud rains its water,
and noble men struggle for other men's good.

65

A sunstone, though insensate,
is incensed when touched by the rays of the sun.
How then can a man of pride
bear slander cast by other men?

66

Authority, renown, protection of priests,
munificence, sensuality, and succor of friends—
when courtiers fail to exhibit these gifts,
what is their worth at the court of a king?

67

He ventures to tether a vicious elephant
with filaments of tender lotus,
to cut an adamantine gem
with petals of silk-tree blossoms,
to render sweet the saline sea
with a single drop of honey,
who tries to lead wicked men to the path of the good
with mellifluous words of wisdom.

68

Creator Brahmā wrought
an extraordinary guise for ignorance,
which may be worn at will.
In company with learned men,
the silence of fools
serves to adorn them.

69

When a man is manifestly wicked
and debauched,
disposed to reckless base behavior
learned through former lives,
an enemy of virtue
whom fate chose to be rich—
why do men take pleasure
in consorting with the boor?

70

Knowledge is man's crowning mark,
a treasure secretly buried,
the source of luxury, fame, and bliss,
a guru most venerable,
a friend on foreign journeys,
the pinnacle of divinity.
Knowledge is valued by kings beyond wealth—
when he lacks it, a man is a brute.

71

Kindness in a kinsman, sympathy in a stranger,
guile in a rogue, affection in a saint,
arrogance in a villain, honesty in a scholar,
prowess in an enemy, patience in a teacher,
cunning in a woman—the skill these people
have in their arts is the basis of society.

72

Giving adorns a man's hand,
homage to teachers his head,
truth his mouth,
valor his conquering arms,
calm composure his heart,
attention to scripture his ears.
Great men endowed with such gems
have no need of princely wealth.

73

The great serpent Śesha
supports the worlds on his hood,
and he in turn is borne
on the back of the tortoise king,
whom the vast ocean shelters
effortlessly in its depths.
The wondrous exploits of the great
exceed all mundane bounds.

74

Whirling through existence,
every man who dies is born again;
but he alone is truly born
whose birth exalts his race.

75

A lion when young makes bold assault
on an elephant in rutting rage.
Daring is born in the valiant;
age and might are not its cause.

76

Armlets do not adorn a person,
or necklaces luminous as the moon;
or ablutions, or ointments,
or blossoms, or beautiful hair.
Eloquent speech that is polished well
really adorns a person—
When other ornaments are ruined,
the ornament of speech is an enduring jewel.

Passionate Encounters

77

Discrimination's lucid light
continues to shine for learned men
only while it is not eclipsed
by the tremulous lashes of women's eyes.

78

When men behold the beauty of women
with exotic flashing eyes,
youthful pride in voluptuous breasts,
creepers of beauty-creases
twining above their slender bellies,
those few are fortunate whose minds
are still unperturbed.

79

With smiles, affection, modesty, and art;
hostile looks and ardent glances;
eloquence, jealous quarrels, and play—
with all her emotions woman enchains us.

80

With the striking of their slipping bangles,
the jeweled sounds of their girdles,
and their ringing anklets,
they shame the call of the royal goose.
With the trembling eyes of frightened does,
whose mind will girls not destroy?

81

I do indeed speak without bias;
this is acknowledged as truth among men.
Nothing enthralls us like an ample-hipped woman;
nothing else causes such pain.

82

Women's gestures are naturally charming,
seductive only in a fool's infatuated heart.
The lotus's passionate red is natural too,
and still bees hover there bewitched.

83

The pleasures of sense may be trivial
and bitter in the end;
they may be spurned and marked
as an abode of evil,
and yet, even the majesty of men
whose thoughts are fixed on truth
wavers in their power.
What force throbs in our hearts?

84

Cut off all envy, examine the matter,
tell us decisively, you noble men,
which we ought to attend upon:
the sloping sides of wilderness mountains
or the buttocks of women abounding in passion?

85

Why all these words and empty prattle?
Only two worlds are worth a man's devotion:
the youth of beautiful women wearied by heavy breasts
and full of fresh wine's excitement,
or the forest.

86

King, who in this world has crossed
to the end of the ocean of craving?
And what is the use of great wealth
when the body's youthful passion is spent?
We frequent a house only as long
as the beauty of its lotuses blooms—
we go often so age will not suddenly
waste our mistresses' shapely form.

87

The sky is dark in a cloak of clouds,
across the hills peacocks dance,
the ground is white with fallen blossoms.
Where does a traveler dare to rest his eye?

88

In this vapid, mundane world,
wise men take two courses:
they spend some time with minds
submerged in the fluid elixir of wisdom,
the rest with tender women
whose breasts and hips enjoy the pleasure
of hiding men's eager hands
in their laps of ample flesh.

89

Lured here by curving beautiful brows,
there by gestures of modesty,
by quivering looks of alarm,
by the graces of amorous play,
by lovely faces and darting eyes—
I am lured by signs of awakening maids
and every direction seems strewn
with lotuses blooming for dalliance.

90

A face to rival the moon,
eyes that make mockery of lotuses,
complexion eclipsing gold's luster,
thick tresses that shame the black bee,
breasts like elephant's swelling temples,
heavy hips,
a voice enchanting and soft—
the adornment in maidens is natural.

91

There is no ambrosia or poison
except in the love of an ample-hipped woman;
enamored, she is an ambrosial vine,
indifferent, a poisonous creeper.

92

Glances cast with dancing brows and downcast eyes,
tender words and modest smiles,
dallying languor in posture and gait—
all are woman's ornament and her weapon.

93

Her smiling mouth,
the power of her artless tremulous glance!
The stream of words
sweet with talk of new diversions!
Her invention of movements
displaying a sapling's lithe grace!
What charm eludes a fawn-eyed maiden
entering into the fullness of youth?

94

Who raised this maze of doubts, house of scandal,
bawdy town of audacity?
Who carved this mine of faults, region of deceits,
sowed this field of sham?
Who built this bar at heaven's gate, aperture to hell's abyss,
wove this hoard of sorcery?
Who contrived the woman-snare, potion of ambrosial poison
fetter for the world of men?

95

A man may tread the righteous path,
be master of his senses,
retire in timidity
or cling to modest ways—only until
the arrow-glances of amorous women
fall on his heart,
glances drawn to her ear,
shot from the bow of her brow,
and winged by long black lashes.

96

Bearing the luster of a full moon
at its loftiest phase,
the lotus-face of a slender girl
locks honey in her lips.
What is tart now like unripe fruit
on vines of gourd,
when time has run its course
will be an acrid poison.

97

How could men of wisdom
let their minds' vigor be sapped,
be distracted by the ignominies of courting
at the gates of an evil king's palace,
were it not for girls' flashing lotus eyes,
splendid as the newly risen moon,
girls with belts of bells playing
on fine waists bent by heavy breasts.

98

Women bathed in sandalwood scents,
flashing antelope-eyes,
arbors of fountains, flowers,
and moonlight,
a terrace swept with breezes
of flowering jasmine—
in summer they stimulate
love and the love-god himself.

99

Winds laden with perfumes,
branches tipped with tender shoots;
mates of cuckoos whose drunken cries
express their longing;
moonlike faces of women
with drops of moisture from sports of love—
how do nature's riches spread
to make such opulence in summer?

100

Even the scholar of scripture,
though his discipline be thorough and his wisdom profound,
rarely partakes of high estate in the world.
The culprit unlocking the door to the city of hell
is fair-eyed woman's key, her graceful creeper-brow.

101

Like waves three furrows of beauty encircle her waist,
a pair of wild geese in flight are her lusty breasts,
a radiant blooming lotus is her face.
Unless you long for the river which bears woman's form
and shelters the monster of her moods, escape
and shun the worldly waters' deadly ablution.

102

A melodious song,
a graceful form,
a sweet draught,
a heady fragrance,
then the touch of her breasts.
I whirl in sensations
which veil what is real.
I fall deceived by senses
cunning in seduction's art.

103

O worldly existence, the path
that leads beyond your bounds
would be less treacherous
were it not for intoxicating glances
waylaying us at every turn.

104

Don't let your wandering mind
stray in the forest of woman's body.
There in the mountains of her breasts
lurks the robber god of love.

105

A cloud drenching the tree of passion,
a torrent of desire seeking love's diversion,
a valued ally of the love-god;
an ocean concealing pearls of cunning,
a waxing moon drunk by woman's thirsting gaze,
a mine of tempting treasure—
youth spares only a favored few
from the crises of its turbulence.

106

It is passion's abode,
the source of a hundred hells of pain,
delusion's seed,
the cloud eclipsing the moon of knowledge,
the love-god's loyal friend,
in league with sundry flagrant sins—
this world boasts no forest
with so many flowers of evil as youth.

107

What is supreme among visions?
The face of a fawn-eyed maid delighted by love.
Among fragrances? the breath of her mouth.
Among sounds? her speech.
Among tastes? the nectar of her budlike lips.
Among textures? her soft body.
What should fill lovers' thoughts
when they are young? her amorous gestures.

108

Surely the moon does not rise in her face,
or a pair of lotuses rest in her eyes,
or gold compose her body's flesh.
Yet, duped by poets' hyperbole, even a sage,
a pondering man, worships the body of woman—
a mere concoction of skin and flesh and bones.

109

To the blind, the ugly, the barren and decrepit man,
to the churl, the man of low birth, and the leper,
they yield their seductive bodies in hope of a trifling sum.
Who can be enamored of courtesans,
knives which slash discernment's wish-granting vine?

110

A courtesan is the fire of passion,
flaming with the fuel of beauty;
a fire where youth and wealth
are sacrificed by lustful men.

111

Through sweet medley of cuckoos' cries
and winds of the sandalwood mountains Spring
destroys creatures estranged from their lovers.
In affliction even nectar turns to poison.

112

We bow to the god whose sign is a sea serpent,
to Love, who makes the gods Shiva, Brahmā, and Vishnu
slaves in dark chambers of doe-eyed women;
to Kāma, whose marvelous artifice eludes all words.

113

Woman is Love's victorious seal,
imprinting his triumph on all things.
Deluded men who forsake her
are fools pursuing illusory fruits,
fools condemned by Love without mercy
to become naked mendicants, wearing shorn,
tufted, or shaggy hair
and bearing begging bowls of skull bone.

114

Guileful Love casts his woman-lure
abroad, into this worldly sea.
Fools greedy for her ruddy lips
are quickly caught like fish
and broiled on passion's flame.

115

When women burn
from zeal of frenzied passion,
even great Brahmā
fears to bar their way.

116

White jasmine in her hair,
the drowsy look of her face,
saffron mixed with sandal paste
on her lovely body—
a mistress with the languor
of seduction in her breasts
is heaven
in its highest sphere.

117

When saffron paste stains her body,
necklaces dangle on her pale yellow breasts,
anklets sound like wild geese on her lotus feet,
what man escapes the enchantress's sway?

118

Surely poets are mistaken
who call amorous women "weak."
When their tremulous wanton glances
captivate heroic gods like Indra,
how can they be weak?

119

Full unruly breast, flashing eyes, enticing brows,
and budlike lips full of passion disquiet me.
Well they may, but why does a supple line of hair
drawn on her waist by Love's flower weapon
become an indelible mark of beauty
to torment me so excessively?

120

A deceiver of himself and his peers
is the pompous pandit who reviles young women.
The fruit of his austerity is heaven,
and even heaven is full of nymphs.

121

A certain slender woman was wandering,
seeking solace in shadows of forest trees,
warding off the moon's scorching rays
with the silken shawl held by her hand.

122

When she is out of sight we long to see her,
beholding her we yearn for sweet embrace,
and when we hold the long-eyed beauty
our bodies crave for union.

123

When she lies on your chest
amid the disarray of her own scented hair,
with eyes like slightly opened buds
and cheeks flushed pink from love's fatigue,
the lips of a woman are honey
which favored men drink.

124

At first she rebuffs me,
then in a mood born of dalliance, passion is roused;
slowly her body falls languid, and composure is shed,
leaving her bold enough to indulge in games of love
played by her limbs' abandoned gestures—
a gentlewoman's pleasure is my delight.

125

A woman is ambrosial
in range of my eyes,
but escaped from my sight,
she surpasses poison.

126

Spells cannot cure it, nor drugs confound it,
nor ritual magic deal it destruction—
passion, like an epileptic fit, attacks man's limbs
to inflict the torment of frenzied derangement.

127

The love-god must be the vassal
of fair-browed woman;
he moves to conquer any man marked
by the course of her glance.

128

It is strange and perverse that men
indulge erotic passion in old age,
and that round-hipped women do not stop
living or loving when their breasts sag.

129

I prefer being bitten by a terrible serpent,
long, wanton, tortuous, gleaming like a black lotus,
to being smitten by her eye.
Healers are everywhere to cure one of a serpent bite,
but there is no spell or remedy for me;
I was struck by the glance of a beautiful woman!

130

Beside a lamp or flaming hearth,
in light of stars or sun or moon—
without her fawnlike eyes
my world remains in darkness.

131

With the moonstone beauty of her face,
her sapphire-black tresses,
her hands the ruby of red lotuses,
she glowed with the magic of gems.

132

With breasts as heavy as Jupiter,
her face radiant as the moon,
her languid legs' saturnine gait,
she glowed with the planets' magic.

133

My girl, you perform a singular feat
with the archer's bow.
You pierce hearts without arrows,
with only the bow-string of beauty.

134

A whitewashed dwelling,
the moon with crystal beams,
the lotus look of a beloved face,
redolent sandal paste,
and garlands of sweet fragrance—
in a man of passion
all this creates unrest,
but not in one who scorns the luxury
of pleasure.

135

Rest yourself on a shore of the Ganges
whose waters ward off sin,
or between the breasts of a maid
whose necklace snares the mind.

136

If her breasts are full,
her hips voluptuous,
her face exquisite,
why, my heart, do you waste in despair?
Earn merit if you covet them!
The luxuries elude a man without merit.

137

Flashing streaks of lightning,
drifting fragrance of tropical pines,
thunder sounding from gathering clouds,
peacocks crying in amorous tones—
how will long-lashed girls pass
these seductive days without their lovers?

138

Beside him his mistress embodying love,
languid from games of abandon.
The cooing of amorous cuckoos in his ears.
A bower of newly blooming creepers.
Conversation with eloquent bards
beneath stray beams of the moon.
The heart of any man here is enchanted
by Spring's varied garlands of color.

139

Your bound-up hair is restrained:
your long eyes stretch
beyond the mundane pale;
the teeth of your mouth
are twice born like noble men and pure;
your breasts which swell like elephants' temples
are a splendid resting place for pearls
released from the oyster's hold.
Lady, though your beauty speaks of peace,
it only incites my passion for you.

140

When clouds shade the sky
and plantain lilies mask the earth,
when winds bear lingering scents
of fresh verbena and kadamba,
and forest retreats rejoice
to the cries of peacocks,
then ardent longing overpowers
loved and wretched men alike.

141

Dressed like a girl in fiery passion,
diffusing the fragrance of blossoming nutmeg,
and bearing heavy swollen clouds,
autumnal rains arouse any man's lust.

142

Heavy rains keep lovers
trapped in their mansions—
in the shivering cold a lord
is embraced by his long-eyed mistress,
and winds bearing cool mists
sooth their fatigue after loveplay.
Even a dreary day is fair
for men who lie in love's arms.

143

Half the night was spent
in the hard embraces of passionate play.
Now, on an isolated porch, his insatiable thirst indulges
in intoxicating draughts,
poured from a water jug by the languid creeper-arm
of his love-wearied mistress.
He is a cursed man who never drinks this autumnal water,
a crystal flow shattered by moonlight.

144

Dining on foods rich in curd, milk, and ghee,
wearing robes of scarlet madder,
warm on their saffron-smeared bodies,
they lie weary from pleasure's diversions,
wrapped in the embrace of voluptuous mistresses
whose mouths are moistened with betel leaf—
favored men lie in winter's ease.

145

Unloosing their hair,
pressing closed their eyes,
pulling at their garments,
exciting chills on their flesh,
destroying their composure,
biting their lips
until great sighs confess their love;
the wind in winter is a lusty lover
of beautiful women.

146

When his mind and his person, through practice of yoga,
hold control over evil passion
and endless benevolence throbs in his heart,
what use has the master ascetic for these:
the prattle of fond women,
honey lips and honey faces,
the sweetness of sighs,
or wanton embrace of heavy breasts?

147

Renunciation of worldly attachment
is only the talk of scholars,
whose mouths are wordy with wisdom.
Who can really forsake the hips
of beautiful women bound
with girdles of ruby jewels?

Refuge in the Forest

148

So I have roamed through perilous lands
in fruitless pursuit of reward,
relinquished my pride and my birthright
to fawn in futile servitude,
shamelessly eaten in other men's homes,
cowering like a common crow.
Greed, you gloated on my wretched deeds;
even now you will not rest content!

149

I mined the earth in search of treasure,
smelted iron mountains' rocky hoards,
crossed treacherous oceans' expanses,
placated kings with devoted care;
bent on evoking occult powers,
by night I roamed the burning grounds.
Not even a broken cowrie shell did I find—
cursed greed, grant me some reprieve!

150

I bear the villains' taunting words
intent upon appeasing them.
I choke my tears, which in disguise
become an empty heart's laughter.
I pay vile homage to my foes
stupefied by wealth.
Hope, you are barren—how
do you still compel me to dance?

151

The cyclic recurrence of sunset and dawn
daily serves to measure life's decay,
but burdened with his mundane tasks,
man does not grasp time's movement;
seeing old age and pain and death,
he does not experience terror.
Drunk on the heady wine of delusion,
the world is mad in oblivion.

152

If other men did not see his wife the pitiful victim
of poverty's woe, and the gaunt faces
of his starved and whimpering children
as they pulled at their mother's ragged clothes,
how could he stammer out the word "give"
that sticks in his throat from fear of rebuff?
What high-minded man would stoop to beg
for the sake of his own empty belly?

153

All desire for pleasure has waned,
the esteem of men has ebbed;
beloved friends and peers of life
now are lost to heaven;
the simplest movement requires a cane;
these eyes are veiled in darkness.
How bold this body is to fear
the final blow of death!

154

I failed to fix my aimless thoughts on Shiva's
holy foot to cleave these mundane bonds;
I heedlessly shunned the righteous way
which penetrates heaven's massive doors;
I even failed in my dreams to embrace
woman's voluptuous breasts, and her ample hips.
I lived my life like an ax, wasting
the forest of youth my mother slaved to nurture.

155

We savored no pleasure,
so we are consumed.
We practiced no penance,
so we are afflicted.
We did not elude time,
so we are pursued.
We did not wither craving,
so we are the wizened.

156

My face is graven with wrinkles,
my hair is streaked with gray,
my limbs are withered and feeble—
my craving alone keeps its youth.

157

Even the sensuous pleasures which rest
within our reach inevitably ebb away.
Is the pain of abstention so intense
that man cannot renounce them himself?
If pleasures abandon him at random,
man suffers unparalleled anguish;
but if he renounces them at will,
he reaps the fruit of eternal calm.

158

Even though my food is alms,
a single meager daily meal;
though my bed is bare ground,
my servant no one but myself;
though my clothes are tattered,
patched with scraps of rag,
the lures of the senses
never grant release.

159

Her breasts, those fleshy protuberances,
are compared to golden bowls;
her face, a vile receptacle of phlegm,
is likened to the moon;
her thighs, dank with urine, are said
to rival the elephant's trunk.
Mark how this despicable form
is flourished by the poets.

160

Unconscious of its violent power,
the moth flies into a flame.
The unwary fish through ignorance
bites the baited hook.
And even we, men who perceive
the tangled net of ruin
which passion casts, do not avoid it.
Alas, delusion's sway is inscrutable!

161

Forest fruits are my only food,
mountain water my drink,
the bare earth my bed,
bark cloth is my raiment.
I cannot acquiesce
in the impudence of evil men
whose drunken senses totter
from the wine of trifling wealth.

162

This world was engendered long ago
by gracious men with noble hearts.
Some sustained it, others conquered
to give it away as if it were straw.
Men of courage even now enjoy power
over the various realms.
What then is this fever of pride
in men who rule the smallest town?

163

You are a king;
I am exalted in homage to an honored guru's wisdom.
You are notorious for your might;
the poets spread my fame across the worlds.
O prince of pride,
the gulf between us is not great.
If you turn your face from me,
I am quite indifferent.

164

When warring rulers never cease
to ravage and divide the land,
what glory is there for a king
in conquest?
But men who rule some meager plot of land,
village lords,
who ought to feel despair,
rather boast delight—the fools!

165

Our intellects are not intent on knavery;
we rank not as dancers, lewd buffoons, or songsters,
nor as women bent with weighty breasts.
Who then are we in the palace of a king?

166

You are a king of opulence;
I am a master
of infinite words.
You are a warrior;
I hold a skill in eloquence
which subdues the fever of pride.
Men blinded by riches serve you;
but they desire to hear me
that their minds may be pure.
Since you have no regard for me,
the less have I for you,
O king—I am gone.

167

Why, my heart, do you waste the days
seeking attention of other men?
Why do you enter the thicket
of anguish just to curry favor?
If you find contentment within yourself,
your thought will become a wish-granting gem—
zeal for freedom's joy
will starve your worldly craving.

168

To cultivate lives as ephemeral
as droplets on a lotus leaf,
what do we not stoop to do
when discrimination fails us?
In front of rich men,
senseless from wines of wealth,
I shamelessly stood boasting
about my own virtues.

169

Alas, my friend, great was the king
with his circle of courtiers,
the counselors at his side,
the ladies' moonlike faces,
the host of haughty princes,
the bards and their tales—
but we submit to time,
which swept them all from power
to the path of memory.

170

Our parents, who begot and bore us
to the world are long since dead.
Our friends of youth are banished
to the realm of memory.
Now, from day to day, we wait for
death's imminent call—
like trees on the frail sandbanks
of rivers, we wait for the flood.

171

In a house that once was full,
a solitary man stands.
Where many descendants lived,
no one remains.
They toss day and night
like a pair of dice
and move men like pawns—
Time plays a frenzied game with Kālī,
his partner in destruction.

172

Should I sojourn in austerity
on the sacred river's bank,
or should I, in worldly fashion,
court women of high grace?
Or drink at streams of scripture
the nectar of rich verse?
In life as transient as a flashing glance,
I can choose no single course.

173

Hope is a river
whose water is desire,
whose waves are craving.
Passions are crocodiles,
conjectures are birds
destroying the tree of resolve.
Anxiety carves a deep ravine
and the whirlpool of delusion
makes it difficult to ford.
Let ascetics who cross
to the opposite shore
exult in their purified minds.

174

Days which dragged through the heavy pain
I felt entreating wealthy lords,
days which fled to naught while my mind
was ensnared in the sensuous sphere—
let me recollect the laughter
of those cursed days' end
when I awake from meditation's depths,
seated on a mountain cave's stone couch.

175

I never learned pure scholarship
or amassed any wealth;
my mind was not devout
in reverence due my parents.
Even in dreams I failed to embrace
maids with trembling eyes.
I passed my time like a common crow
groveling for other men's crumbs.

176

Though I search the triple world
through all its mundane passages,
no man has met my vision's field
or come within my hearing's range
who could really bind
to a post of self-restraint
the raging elephant of his mind
with its drunken desire to court
the world of the senses.

177

I dwell content in the hermit's dress of bark,
while you luxuriate in silken splendor.
Still, my contentment is equal to yours;
disparity's guise is deceiving.
Now let him be called a pauper
who bears an insatiable greed;
when a mind rests content,
what can it mean to be "wealthy" or "poor"?

178

Pleasures are as ephemeral as lightning
flashing through a canopy of clouds;
life is as fragile as a water-filled
thunderhead blown by the wind;
transient for mortals is youth's caressing.
Wise men, reflect on this and hasten
to fix your minds in yoga,
purest fruit of calm and trance.

179

Wandering through holy cities or sacred forests,
bearing the covered alms bowl,
begging where the smoke-gray sky
gives sign that priests offer holy oblations
whose remnants are fit for mendicants—
this is the righteous way
to fill a gnawing belly.
The proud mendicant is still blessed,
but not the parasitic wretch
who grovels daily amid his kinsmen.

180

Abandon the depths of sensuous chaos,
that prison of torment!
The course reaching beyond toward bliss
can instantly allay all pain.
Initiate then a peaceful mood!
Renounce your gamboling unsteady ways!
Forsake the ephemeral mundane passions!
Rest placid now, my thoughts!

181

My dear, rest content
with forest flowers, herbs, and fruits;
with earth's bare couch
and garments fashioned crudely of fresh bark.
We retire now to a sylvan silence,
to the forest where no echo sounds
of wicked men whose muddled minds
show their confusion—
vile lords whose tongues stammer folly aloud,
confounded by disease of wealth.

182

Purge your delusion,
find joy in moon-crested Shiva,
dwell in devotion, my thoughts,
on the banks of the heavenly river!
What certainty exists in waves, or bubbles,
or streaks of lightning?
In women, or flames, or serpents,
or torrents of water?

183

Songs sound before you, eloquent bards
from the south are at your side,
behind you are plume-bearing maids
whose anklets ring in play.
If you so desire,
taste these worldly delights.
If not, my mind, plunge into
deep meditation, into a trance
free from fantasy dilemmas.

184

Are roots extinct in the valleys?
Have mountain cascades ceased to fall?
Are boughs that bear fruit and yield
the hermit's bark withered on the trees?
How can the world bear to behold
the faces of arrogant rogues
whose brows dance in the winds
of a little hard-won wealth?

185

O beneficent Shiva,
behold a solitary man,
free from desire, tranquil,
drinking from his hands,
wearing the sky as his raiment.
When shall I master the way
to root out the store of my karma?

186

If wealth which yields all desire is won,
what then?
If your foot stands on the head of your foes,
what then?
If honored men are drawn to you by riches' force,
what then?
If man's mundane body endures for an aeon,
what then?

187

When man feels devotion to the Lord Shiva,
has the fear in his heart of death and rebirth,
indulges no bonds of attachment to kinsmen
or frenzy born of amorous passion;
when he dwells in a lonely forest
free from the taints of society,
he lives indifferent to worldly concerns.
What loftier goal can man strive to attain?

188

If you men perceive your deeper selves,
then reach toward Brahman boundless,
enduring, remote, and pervading;
and it shall follow that
power and pleasure in the world
will seem the obsessions of wretched fools.

189

You descend to nether worlds,
you traverse the sky,
you roam the horizon
with such mobility, my mind!
Why do you never, even in error,
remember what is pure
and part of yourself,
that Brahman, through which
you would reach your final bliss?

190

Earth his soft couch,
arms of creepers his pillow,
the sky his canopy,
tender winds his fan,
the moon his brilliant lamp,
indifference his mistress,
detachment his joy—
tranquil, the ash-smeared hermit
sleeps in ease like a king.

191

Why do men need scriptures revealed, remembered,
recited in legend? Why tedious tomes of precepts?
Why the labyrinth of ritual acts
performed for reward in heaven's abode?
When compared with the fire ending time,
ending all the pain of worldly toil,
and leading men's souls into bliss,
all these are the goods of haggling merchants.

192

Life is a rough uncertain wave.
The splendor of youth is a transient bloom.
Fortune is imagination's whim.
Pleasure flashes like lightning during the rains.
Even fond embraces of beloved arms
do not rest long in their show of love.
Meditate then on that highest Brahman
to cross beyond this sea of worldly dread.

193

Moonlight beams, a forest glade,
the fellowship of friends,
the legends told in poetry,
all are enchanting.
Enchanting too is her lovely face
gleaming with tears of anger—
enchanting if only your thought can forget
their ephemeral nature.

194

While his body's vigor is whole
and old age is remote;
while his sensuous powers are unimpaired
and life not yet exhausted;
only then will a wise man
strive to perfect his soul.
Why attempt to dig a well
when the house is already burning?

195

I failed to master the knowledge
needed to conquer the host of polemists
abroad in the world.
I did nothing to spread my fame
across the sky on the rapier
made to pierce war elephants' heads.
I never sipped the moonrise nectar
from women's beautiful,
tender, blossom lips.
Alas, I passed a futile youth,
like a flaming lamp
in an empty house.

196

You are favored men who sit in mountain caves,
in meditation on an inner light,
while on your laps calmly perch birds of prey
to drink the tears of bliss.
But we, poor fools,
waste away our lives in games,
dallying in pleasure ·groves and ponds
of castles desire creates.

197

Birth is scented with death.
Youth's brilliance is shadowed by old age.
Contentment is menaced by ambition,
calm, by impudent women's amorous looks,
virtues, by men's malice,
woodlands, by serpents, and kings, by villains.
Rich treasure
is plundered by transience.
Is anything spared the threat of eclipse?

198

Youth in its prime is sapped
by a hundred plagues of longing.
Wherever the bird of wealth alights,
misfortunes swarm through open gates.
Soon death is sovereign
over every helpless creature born.
What is fashioned to endure
through capricious fate?

199

Still unborn, man suffers a painful
confinement in woman's foul womb.
In youth, he suffers separation's pangs,
the misery of each parting
lover's embrace.
Even old age is accursed,
exposing him to women
flashing looks of scorn.
Tell me, men, does worldly existence
offer us any joy at all?

200

The span of man's life is a measured hundred yea
yet half is lost to night
and of his waking time,
callow youth and hoary age each claim a share;
his prime is spent in servitude, suffering
the anguish of estrangement and disease.
Where do men find happiness
in life less certain and more transient than the wa

❧ BILHANA'S POEMS ❧

Fantasies of a Love-Thief

1

Even now,
I regret her—
gleaming in garlands of gold champac flowers,
her lotus face blossoming,
the line of down delicate at her waist,
her body trembling and eager for love
when she wakes from sleep—
magic I lost somehow in recklessness.

2

Even now,
if I see her again,
her full moon face, lush new youth,
swollen breasts, passion's glow,
body burned by fire from love's arrows—
I'll quickly cool her limbs!

3

Even now,
if I see her again,
a lotus-eyed girl
weary from bearing her own heavy breasts—
I'll crush her in my arms
and drink her mouth like a madman,
a bee insatiably drinking a lotus!

4

Even now,
I remember her in love—
her body weak with fatigue,
swarms of curling hair
falling on pale cheeks,
trying to hide
the secret of her guilt.
Her soft arms
clung
like vines on my neck.

5

Even now,
I remember her:
deep eyes' glittering pupils
dancing wildly in love's vigil,
a wild goose
in our lotus bed of passion—
her face bowed low with shame
at dawn.

6

Even now,
if I see her again,
wide-eyed,
fevered from long parting—
I'll lock her tight in my limbs,
close my eyes, and never leave her!

7

Even now,
I remember her
holding the reins
in our wild dance of love,
moon luster lighting her face,
her body trembling with passion—
delicate,
bent by lush breasts and heavy hips,
dancing mantled in a mane of flying hair.

8

Even now,
I remember her lying in bed,
spreading perfume of musk
mixed with sandalwood oils—
her seductive eyes' lashes playing
like a pair of mating birds
caressing each others' bills.

9

Even now,
I remember the wine-smeared lips
she innocently licked in love,
her frail form, her wanton long eyes,
her body rubbed golden
with saffron paste and musk,
her mouth spiced
with camphor and betel nut.

10

Even now,
at the end, I remember my love's face
colored with shining saffron powder,
covered with sweat drops,
with love-weary tremulous eyes—
a moon disc
released by the demon eclipse.

11

Even now,
my mind dwells on the night
my sneezing awoke the princess.
Flustered, she refused to say
"Jīva—Long life!"
Silently, she put
a lucky golden charm on her ear.

12

Even now,
I remember my love's face:
golden earrings
grazing her cheeks
as she strove
to take the man's role,
beads of sweat strewn thick
like pearls
from the toil
of her rhythmic swinging.

13

Even now,
I remember her bold bent glance,
her graceful limbs stretching
in pleasure,
her voluptuous breasts' curve
bared by slipping clothes,
her lip bruised with marks of my teeth.

14

Even now,
I remember my love:
hands painted red
like young leaves of ashoka,
tips of breasts
caressed by ropes of pearls,
pale cheeks
freshened by hidden smiles,
her languourous wild-goose gait.

15

Even now,
I remember the mark my nail left
on her sandalwood-powdered thigh—
the gold-streaked cloth I snatched
when she rose
was clutched in shame as she pulled away.

16

Even now,
I remember in secret
her kohl-lined longing eyes,
flower-heavy plaited hair,
vermilion lips
framing her teeth's pearl luster,
arms bound by golden bracelets.

17

Even now,
I remember in secret
her braid's loosened ties,
wilted garlands,
nectar-sweet smiling lips,
strands of pearls
caressing luscious swollen breasts,
and longing looks.

18

Even now,
I brood on her:
when streaks of light from jeweled lamps
broke the darkness in her white pavilion,
I seized the chance to stare at her secretly—
her eyes flashed with shame and fear.

19

Even now,
I remember her,
a fragile fawn-eyed girl,
her body burning with fires of parted love,
ready for my passion—
a beauty moving like a wild goose,
bringing me rich ornaments.

20

Even now,
I remember my love
gently laughing,
bent by heavy breasts,
dazzling in ropes of pearls—
a banner of open blossoms
flown by flower-armed Love
high on the mountain of passion.

21

Even now,
I remember a hundred flatteries
spoiling the sense of her words
when she trembled in exhaustion after love—
the sweet words came in jumbled sounds
she whispered faintly, timidly spoke.

22

Even now,
I remember her eyes
trembling, closed after love,
her slender body limp,
fine clothes and heavy hair loose—
a wild goose
in a thicket of lotuses of passion.
I'll remember her in my next life
and even at the end of time!

23

Even now,
if I see her again at the day's close,
adoring me with a fawn's liquid eyes
and offering her breasts' brimming pots of nectar—
I'll renounce kingly pleasures
and even heaven's highest bliss!

24

Even now,
I remember her,
the ideal of amorous women on earth
through the beauty of her body,
the perfect cup for tasting nectar
in the play of passion—
my girl, wounded by Love's flower arrows.

25

Even now,
I never forget her,
clinging to my limbs like wet cloth
when her body burned
with fires of love's violent passion—
pitiful now without her lover's protection,
my girl makes mockery of life.

26

Even now,
I remember her,
first among beautiful women,
an exquisitely molded vessel for passion—
the king's daughter pleading,
"People, I can't bear this fire of parting!"

27

Even now,
knowing death is quickly closing in,
my thought leaves the gods,
is drawn to her in wonder. What can I do?
I am obsessed: "She is my love!
Most beloved! She is mine!"

28

Even now,
in pain I recall her eyes
trembling like a frightened deer's
when she heard my sentence pronounced—
her quavering voice,
tears falling from her eyes,
her face bowed by heavy grief.

29

Even now,
though I strain my vision,
I can't find a face to rival my love's—
its brilliance is blinding, eclipsing
the moon and the beauty of love's consort.

30

Even now,
I remember her,
a poison in short separations,
in reunion ablutions of nectar—
my life's sustainer,
my shield from the burns of love,
is a beautiful girl's rich mane.

31

Even now,
I shudder to face
what she tried for my sake—
and still the messengers of Death,
hard, terrible hands,
dragged me from her rooms.

32

Even now,
my heart suffers night and day.
I'll never again see
my love's beautiful full moon face,
glowing with a salty beauty
that dulls the nectar
of night-blooming jasmine.

33

Even now,
my haunted mind broods on her—
forbidden girl, my life's hope,
rich with fresh youth
no one now enjoys—
let her be my fate in another life too!

34

Even now,
the sound of bangles
strikes my mind sharply:
when black bees, wild in their desire
for perfume from her lotus mouth,
swarmed to kiss her cheeks,
her fingers shook them from her hair.

35

Even now,
I remember her bristling in delight
when I was so drunk
from drinking her mouth's sweet wine
that I left a nail mark on her breast—
she stared, studied, treasured the mark.

36

Even now,
I remember her angered face,
her frank impatience to leave
as she sullenly gave me her mouth—
I kissed it; she wept violently.
I fell at her feet:
"I'm your slave, my love! Love me!"

37

Even now,
my mind finds me idling with her friends,
embracing her lovely limbs,
bantering, and dancing
in elegant rooms alive with our play—
If only my time could pass there!

38

Even now,
I don't know!
Is she Shiva's mate,
or a nymph come to earth by Indra's curse,
or Krishna's consort, Lakshmī?
Did Brahmā create her to beguile the world,
or was he driven by desire
to behold the perfect jewel of maiden youth?

39

Even now,
who in the world can paint her form?
It reveals itself, like a creature of fantasy,
only for me.
An aspiring artist would have to see its equal—
and only then begin to try.

40

Even now,
I see her kohl-blackened eyes,
burning mouth,
laughter-weary ears.
I see her body weakened
by its own swelling breasts—
if it wastes away, who is to blame?

41

Even now,
gleaming white like a clear autumn moon,
her luscious face
could charm a saint's pure mind—
it enraptures mine!
If I find it, I'll kiss it
and keep drinking lest it slip from me.

42

Even now,
I would give my life
to recover love's sanctum—
fragrant with lotus pollen,
wet with the semen of passion,
downfall of the love god.

43

Even now,
in a world rich with signs of beauty
surpassing each other's perfections,
my heart believes
that her form is beyond compare.

44

Even now,
a wild goose's plump body
glides on waves she stirs
in a wooded river-cove in my mind—
she is pleading some fatigue
from a fleeting touch
of fine kadamba flower pollen.

45

Even now,
I miss her eyes languidly roving
in their youthful wanton way—
the king's daughter
seemed like a creature from heaven,
the fallen child of celestial singers,
genii, demigods, musicians,
or serpent spirits.

46

Even now,
night and day,
I can't forget her waking from sleep—
her curving form made her waist an altar,
her breasts swelled like pots
brimming with nectar,
her body shone with richly colored ornaments.

47

Even now,
I remember
her languid body rising to a golden glow,
though shame compelled her to pretend exhaustion—
folly broken
as our touching limbs and kisses
left her wanton, like wild life-giving herbs.

48

Even now,
I remember the love-play battle
she fought with empty hands
in rising falling rhythms,
wet with hot red blood
from tooth marks on her lips
and nail marks on her body—
her tyranny bewitched me in the bout.

49

Even now,
how can I endure the loss
of my young mistress's gifts?
Only death will cure my pain.
Brothers, I beg you, end it quickly!

50

Even now,
Shiva does not avoid the sea's black poison.
The Tortoise bears the earth on his back.
The Ocean endures insatiable submarine fires.
The faithful keep the promises they make.

49

Even now,
now can I endure the loss
of my young mistress's grace?
Only death will cure my pain.
Brother, I beg you, end it quickly!

50

Even now,
Shiva does not avoid the sea's black poison,
The Tortoise bears the earth on his back,
The Ocean endures insatiable submarine fire,
The faithful keep the promises they make.